D1164688

The

LIGHTHOUSE FAMILY

THE BEAR

The
LIGHTHOUSE FAMILY

THE BEAR

BY CYNTHIA RYLANT
ILLUSTRATED BY PRESTON McDANIELS

BEACH LANE BOOKS
New York   London   Toronto   Sydney   New Delhi

BEACH LANE BOOKS
An imprint of Simon & Schuster Children's Publishing Division
1230 Avenue of the Americas, New York, New York 10020

For information about special discounts for bulk purchases, please contact Simon &
Schuster Special Sales at 1-866-506-1949 or business@simonandschuster.com.
The Simon & Schuster Speakers Bureau can bring authors to your live event.
For more information or to book an event, contact the Simon & Schuster Speakers
Bureau at 1-866-248-3049 or visit our website at www.simonspeakers.com.
The text for this book was set in Centaur.
The illustrations for this book were rendered in graphite.
Manufactured in the United States of America
0218 PCH
First Edition
2 4 6 8 10 9 7 5 3 1
Library of Congress Cataloging-in-Publication Data
Names: Rylant, Cynthia, author. | McDaniels, Preston, illustrator.
Title: The bear / by Cynthia Rylant ; illustrated by Preston McDaniels.
Description: First edition. | New York : Beach Lane Books, [2018] |
Series: The lighthouse family ; [8] | Summary: After a long winter, the mice Whistler
and Lila invite a sleepy bear to have breakfast at the lighthouse, but when he falls asleep
in the garden for forty-three days, they realize he might not be done hibernating.
Identifiers: LCCN 2017015041 | ISBN 9781481460286 (hardback) |
ISBN 9781481460309 (e-book)
Subjects: | CYAC: Bears—Fiction. | Hibernation—Fiction. | Animals—Fiction. |
Lighthouses—Fiction. | Seashore—Fiction. | BISAC: JUVENILE FICTION /
Animals / Mice, Hamsters, Guinea Pigs, etc.. | JUVENILE FICTION /
Family / General (see also headings under Social Issues). |
JUVENILE FICTION / Action & Adventure / General.
Classification: LCC PZ7.R982 Be 2018 | DDC [Fic]—dc23
LC record available at https://lccn.loc.gov/2017015041

For Addison and Elliott

—*P. McD.*

Contents

1. *Winter Winds*

Lighthouse-keeping can be a

very lonely life, and so it was for Pandora the cat for many years. She had steadily kept the lights burning to warn the sailing ships away from the rocks at the edge of the shore. But Pandora wished, every day, for some company.

Then one day company arrived. A great storm blew a battered little boat named *Adventure* onto shore. And along with this little boat came its sailor, also battered by the sea. His name was Seabold.

Pandora brought Seabold into her cottage next to the lighthouse, and she set right away to tending his broken leg and strengthening him with stew.

In time Seabold was completely well again, and he knew that he must set sail. His life had always been the sea.

But before Seabold sailed away, a different kind of company altogether arrived at the lighthouse, changing everything.

They were Whistler, Lila, and Tiny, three orphaned children drifting helplessly in a crate at sea when Pandora and Seabold found them. The children were quite lost and very hungry.

Pandora and Seabold took care of these children, and because he grew so deeply fond of them, Seabold realized he could not sail away at all.

And together they all became the lighthouse family.

Summer was fun and fall was beautiful, but winter at the lighthouse was *challenging*.

The sky and the sea were always gray and the winter gales blew endlessly. Lighthouse-keeping became very hard work. Pandora and Seabold not only kept a fire going in the kitchen day and night, but they also kept the lamps burning in the light-house tower day and night. They filled the lamps and trimmed the wicks and cleaned the windows of the lantern room constantly. They took turns ringing the fog bell through the night to warn ships to steer away.

Whistler and Lila wanted to help ring the bell,

but Pandora would not allow it. At times the wind blew so fiercely that even she and Seabold had to tie themselves to a tree so they wouldn't blow away.

So the children kept themselves busy with inside things, like playing checkers and teaching Tiny her numbers and letters.

They all caught winter colds, and they rubbed bee balm salve onto their red noses and drank quite a lot of ginger tea.

But finally the winter storms became fewer and fewer. And some mornings there was hardly any fog at all, and everyone knew that spring was tip-toeing in.

One day Whistler and Lila begged Pandora and Seabold to allow them to take a walk.

"We will bundle up three times thicker," promised Lila.

"And we'll cover our noses," added Whistler.

Pandora and Seabold agreed that it would be safe for the children to go, as long as they avoided the windy cliffs and stayed close to the forest's edge.

Seabold handed Whistler a small hourglass.

"One hour only," Seabold said. "Then home."

"One hour only," promised Whistler and Lila.

And as the children stepped outside into the cold air, they both hoped they might be lucky enough to have a one-hour adventure.

2. The Deep Hole

The forest that grew down to the sea cliffs was thick with green ferns and mosses and the fragrance of cedar. Whistler and Lila loved it. But the forest was miles deep. The children knew that without a compass to guide them, they must not venture in but stay on the edge as they had promised.

"What is that?" Whistler asked, pointing to something up ahead. It looked like a little house.

As they drew closer, the children realized it was, in fact, a little house. It was made of sticks and was most impressive, and on its porch sat a wood rat enjoying a cup of tea.

"Good morning," the rat said.

"Good morning," Whistler and Lila answered together.

The rat graciously invited them to join him for tea.

But with only an hour for exploring, the children politely declined.

"Another time!" the rat said cheerfully.

Whistler and Lila continued walking. And it was when they were carefully gathering cloud-berries from some bushes beside a hemlock tree that Whistler became curious about something new.

A deep dark hole had been made by the large roots of the tree, and from this hole a wisp of vapor was rising. It looked just like Whistler's frosty breath.

"Lila," said Whistler, "I believe something in that hole is breathing. See?" Whistler pointed to the vapor mist coming from within the hole.

Lila was cautious.

"It might be a skunk," she said. "Let's ask Seabold."

Whistler did not want to startle a skunk, so they quietly went on with their walk.

The children arrived back at the cottage with only a few minutes left in the hourglass. They told Seabold about the frosty vapor coming from the hole.

"It is probably a hibernating bear," Seabold said.

"A bear!" said Whistler and Lila together.

The children had never met a bear.

Their one-hour walk had proved to be an adventure after all.

Maybe there would be more to come.

3. Someone Wakes Up

While the bear continued his winter sleep under the tree roots, Whistler and Lila visited him with gifts. On clear days they walked to the forest's edge and placed small things just inside his hole: a dried sea fan, an extra checker, a pot holder Lila had made, and, most important, a triton shell they had found in summer. They did not often find those. Triton shells were special.

They also left a note inviting him to breakfast when he woke up. And finally, one chilly spring morning, the bear did wake up.

Because he was so hungry and much too sleepy to find his own breakfast, he stumbled to the cottage beside the lighthouse and knocked on the door.

Pandora opened the door to see a very rumpled furry face with dark, sleepy eyes.

The bear handed her the note and, as politely as possible without yawning too much, he said,

"My name is Thomas, and I believe I am invited for breakfast."

Pandora welcomed Thomas inside. The children came running. They were thrilled!

Pandora made Thomas breakfast, which turned out to be an amazing thirty-four bearberry pancakes. Bears are very hungry when they wake up.

Seabold then invited Thomas to see Pandora's garden.

Being a courteous bear, Thomas said, "I would like that very much."

He yawned a very big yawn.

"Oh, pardon me," he said.

The bear walked all around Pandora's garden, which had many flowers just coming into bud and bloom. Then he spotted the hammock.

"May I?" he asked Seabold.

"Indeed," said Seabold.

Whistler, Lila, Seabold, and Tiny (in the roll of Seabold's cap) watched as the bear eased himself into the hammock.

"*Aaah*," said the bear, very full of pancakes.

He then turned onto his side and instantly went back to sleep.

"Oh dear," said Lila.

The family adjusted. They put a blanket over him on chilly nights. And a tea towel on his head if the sun was bright. Tiny liked to pat his big nose.

Thomas the bear slept in the hammock in Pandora's garden for forty-three days.

4. Thomas Goes Home

Finally Thomas woke up. He was very embarrassed to find he was a guest who had greatly overstayed his welcome.

But the family assured him he had been no trouble at all. And Pandora again fed him thirty-four bearberry pancakes.

After Thomas left the lighthouse, he tidied himself and moved his things onto a very nice ledge beneath a small waterfall, for the view. Then he invited the lighthouse family to his new home.

"Aren't you afraid you might roll off when napping?" Lila asked Thomas as she peered over the ledge.

"Yes," said Thomas. "So I always put a rock beside me. I have not rolled off once."

"Smart!" said Whistler.

"There are rainbows in the waterfall on sunny days," Thomas said with some pride in his voice.

"Such a lovely home," said Pandora. Pandora appreciated good home design.

Thomas invited everyone to share a big bowl of berries. Then, during their visit, the wood rat

stopped by. It turned out that he and Thomas were old friends. In fact, the wood rat had built Thomas's breakfast table.

"Very fine work," said Seabold with admiration.

As the lighthouse family was preparing to return home, Thomas brought forth a surprise.

"The triton shell!" said Whistler.

Thomas pointed to a freshly made hole in the top of the shell.

"A woodpecker did me a small favor," said Thomas.

Then he put the shell to his mouth and played a tune on it!

"Amazing!" cried the children.

Thomas handed the shell to Seabold.

"I will listen for music from your family," Thomas said.

So all through the spring, as the bees woke up and the hummingbirds flew in from the south and the goldenrod bloomed, the lovely sound of music

could be heard coming from the lighthouse on the cliff. The notes floated out and across the sea.

And, sometimes, a humpback whale who loved to sing even answered.

CYNTHIA RYLANT lives in Oregon, not far from the Pacific Ocean, and PRESTON McDANIELS lives on the Great Plains in Aurora, Nebraska.